jj Whitehead, K

LOOKING FOR UNCLE LOUIE
ON THE FOURTH OF JULY

Looking for Uncle Louie on the Fourth of July

BY Kathy Whitehead   ILLUSTRATED BY Pablo Torrecilla

BOYDS MILLS PRESS

The publisher wishes to thank Dr. Mario Barrera, Professor Emeritus, Department of Ethnic Studies, University of California, Berkeley, and Ralph Fuentes, Editor, *Lowrider* magazine, for their assistance in the development of this book.

NOTE
A lowrider is a customized car with a chassis that has been modified to ride low to the ground. Lowriders often feature hydraulic lifts, which are controlled by the driver. With these lifts, the driver is able to raise or lower the chassis as the car drives along, giving it a low stance and new look.

Published by Boyds Mills Press, Inc.
A Highlights Company
815 Church Street
Honesdale, Pennsylvania 18431
Printed in China
Visit our Web site at www.boydsmillspress.com

Library of Congress Cataloging-in-Publication Data

Whitehead, Kathy, 1957–
  Looking for Uncle Louie on the Fourth of July / by Kathy Whitehead ; illustrated by Pablo Torrecilla.—1st ed.
      p. cm.
  Summary: A boy gets a big surprise when the lowriders take part in the Independence Day parade.
  ISBN 1-59078-061-2 (alk. paper)
  [1. Uncles—Fiction. 2. Fourth of July—Fiction. 3. Parades—Fiction. 4. Lowriders—Fiction.
5. Texas—Fiction.] I. Torrecilla, Pablo, ill. II. Title.

  PZ7.W58513Lo 2004   [E]—dc22

2004010781

First edition, 2005
The text of this book is set in 16-point Americana.
The illustrations are done in acrylics and have been digitally enhanced.
10 9 8 7 6 5 4 3 2 1

For Bill, Jeffrey, and Stephanie
—K. W.

To all my American friends,
with best wishes
—P. T.

Crowds line the street to wait
for the Fourth of July parade.
Grownups relax in lawn chairs
while we perch on coolers for a better view.

Relatives are everywhere,
laughing, talking,
and telling jokes.
But I don't see Uncle Louie.

He calls me Big Joe and
lets me wear his cowboy hat.

"Where is Uncle Louie?" I ask, tugging on Mom's shirt.
"That Louie," says Mom, unpacking our lunch.
"He's got a big surprise for you.
Keep your eyes and ears open wide."

I crane my neck to look around,
but I don't see Uncle Louie.

Soldiers proudly carry the red, white, and blue.
I stand tall and give my best salute.
The sailboats in the harbor seem to do the same,
the wind pushing their sails in stiff gusts.

A high-school band marches by next,
twirlers out front,
flinging batons in the air.
The strains of "America the Beautiful" tickle my ears.

I wave to them all,
but I don't see Uncle Louie.

Sashaying dancers in boots and bandanas,
twirl their partners across a wagon floor.
The celebration of our nation
with a south Texas twist.

A *conjunto* band rides by,
their "Star-Spangled Banner"
is hot like jalapeños,
ripe from the scorching Texas sun.

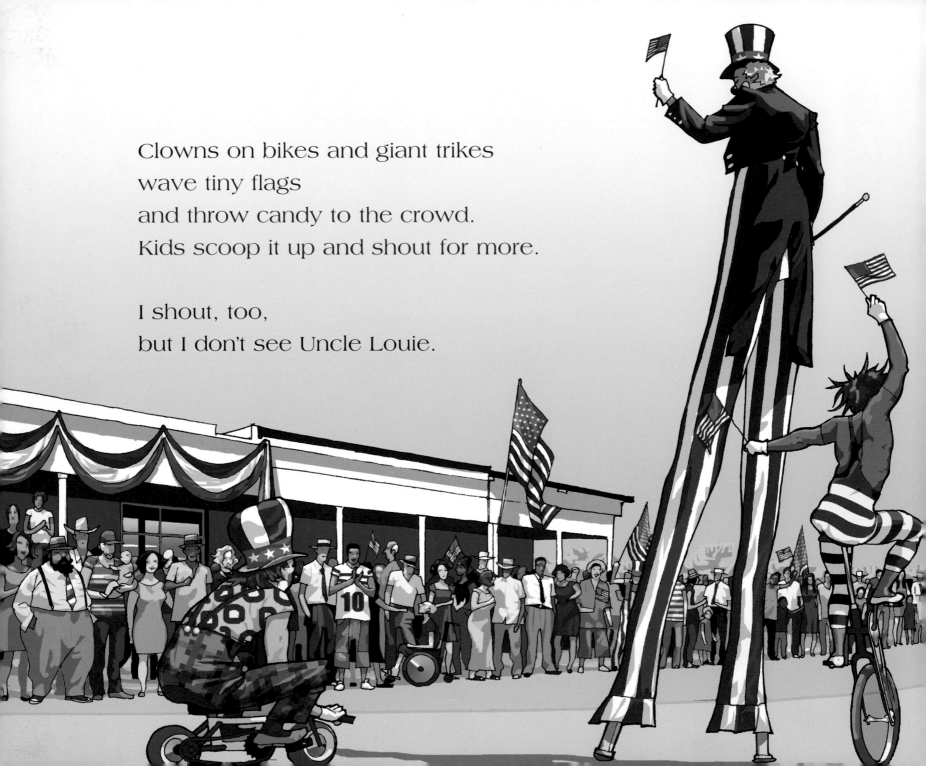

Clowns on bikes and giant trikes
wave tiny flags
and throw candy to the crowd.
Kids scoop it up and shout for more.

I shout, too,
but I don't see Uncle Louie.

Horses prance by,
manes braided and tails brushed.
Their lady riders sit sidesaddle,
full skirts flowing in the breeze.

I keep my eyes and ears open wide.
A rumble grows from down the street.
Could it be Uncle Louie?
I shade my eyes and look.

A flash of chrome blinds me,
as my ears catch a Tejano beat.

A purple lowrider slinks into sight,
pink lightning down the side.
It hugs the ground in front,
while the back floats high above the street.

I wave at the riders in the car.
Lowriders are the best!

A sparkling yellow Chevy follows close behind,
balancing on three wheels
like a tightrope walker,
giving the crowd a big-top thrill.

Behind it purrs a long, low car,
Lady Liberty painted on the hood,
and eight flags flapping, front to back,
on this star-spangled ride.

The driver sports a cowboy hat banded
with the red, white, and blue.
Underneath its turned-up brim,
I spot a familiar lopsided grin.
"Hey, Uncle Louie!"

The car shudders to a halt,
Uncle Louie pops out and opens the door.
He's waving me inside!
Mom nods and smiles as I dive into the big backseat.

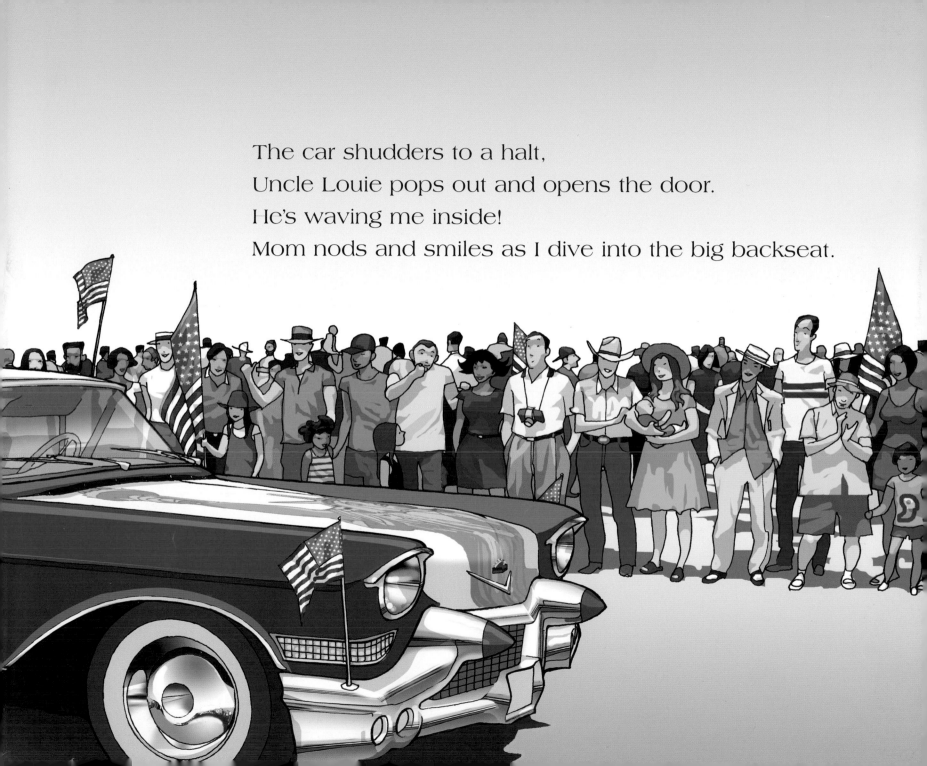

The front bumper starts a stately rise,
a lowrider salute to our nation's birth.
I cheer and sing, glad to be a part
of this star-spangled celebration of our nation.

And best of all, I found my Uncle Louie!